image
Reading for Fun
图像：阅读乐趣

Patricia Landry

Illustrations
Benoît Perroud

商务印书馆
The Commercial Press

Contents 目录

Originally published in English and French by Bordas under the title:
imagier Anglais Français
© 2005 Bordas
Adaptation and translation
© 2006 The Commercial Press (Hong Kong) Ltd.

Name of the Original Book: *imagier Anglais Français*
Author: Patricia Landry
Illustrations: Benoît Perroud

书　　名：**Image : Reading for Fun 图像：阅读乐趣**
编　　著：Patricia Landry
责任编辑：黄家丽
绘　　图：Benoît Perroud
封面设计：张　毅
出　　版：商务印书馆（香港）有限公司
　　　　　香港筲箕湾耀兴道 3 号东汇广场 8 楼
　　　　　http://www.commercialpress.com.hk
总 代 理：商务印书馆（新）有限公司
The Commercial Press (S) Pte Ltd
211 Henderson Road, #05-04 Henderson Industria Park
Singapore 159552
Tel: 6278 3535　Fax: 6278 6300

商务印书馆（马）有限公司
K. L. Commercial Book Co (M) Sdn Bhd
51 Jalan Sultan, 50000 Kuala Lumpur, Malaysia
Tel: 03-20315368　Fax: 03-2031 5143
印　　刷：中华商务彩色印刷有限公司
　　　　　香港新界大埔汀丽路 36 号中华商务印刷大厦
版　　次：2006 年 5 月第 1 版第 1 次印刷
© 2006 商务印书馆（香港）有限公司
ISBN 13 - 978 962 07 1779 6
ISBN 10 - 962 07 1779 1
Printed in Hong Kong

Notes to the Parents 给家长的话

要鼓励孩子开口讲英语，在生活里"就地取材"是其中一种有效的学习方法。无论孩子是在家里，在学校里，还是在街上逛，他们每天所接触的人和事，其实都是练习讲英语的好材料。

本书提供30个生活主题，包括：家庭（The Family）、上学去（Going to School）、在街上（On the Street）、在超级市场购物（Shopping at the Supermarket）、面部表情和感觉（Faces and Feelings）、交通工具（Transport）、游乐场（The Playground）以及运（Sports）等等。每个主题占一个对页的篇幅，一共收录了1,000多个英语单词和惯用语。

最直接的学习方法，是让孩子看图认字，用英语说出事物的名称，打好词汇根基。但本书不仅仅是一本学习词汇的书，还帮助孩子学会讲简单的口语，而家长可以跟孩子一起练习对话，例如家长问：What do you like?，孩子按自己的兴趣回答：I like to play hide and seek. 或 I like to ride a bicycle.。而每章左下角的"亲子学习提示"，可帮助家长引起英语话题，比如家长可指着图问：What's the weather like?，孩子看图回答：It's windy. 然后再叫孩子按真实情况形容今天的天气：What's the weather like today? 这样一问一答，有助孩子学会搭配词语，正确讲出短句。

本书配 CD 一张，由外籍人士录制，朗诵每章的短诗，如 Ready? Go! Ride and swim, we love it so! Jump and run, that's real fun! 孩子一边听，一边学，朗朗上口，便于记忆，不但有助认识英语的节奏、韵律和语调，也有效培养孩子对英语的语感，提高发音及聆听能力。

The House/At Home
房子／在家里

a block of flats (GB) /
an apartment building (US)
一座公寓

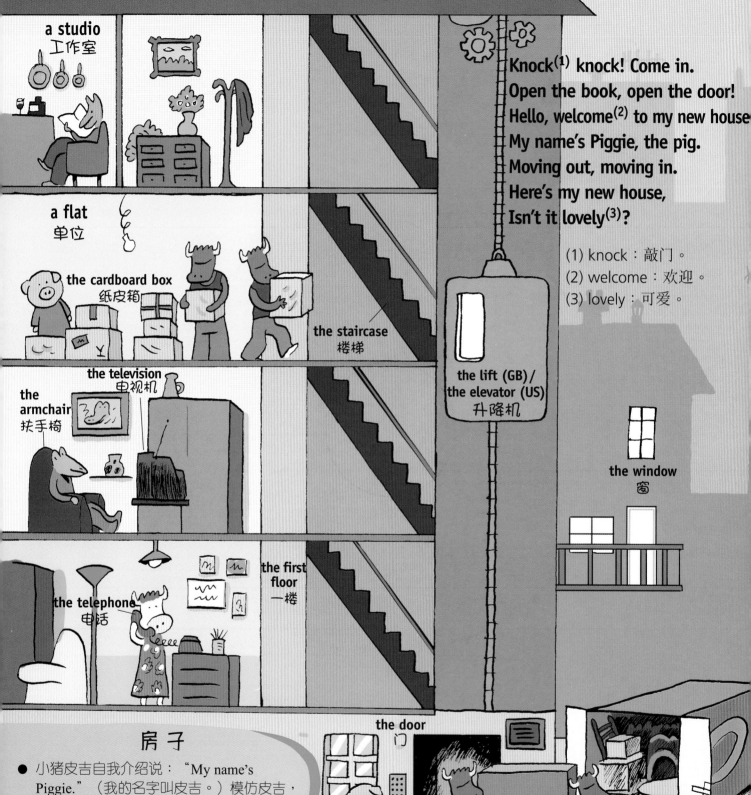

a studio
工作室

a flat
单位

the cardboard box
纸皮箱

the staircase
楼梯

the television
电视机

the armchair
扶手椅

the lift (GB) /
the elevator (US)
升降机

the window
窗

the telephone
电话

the first
floor
一楼

the door
门

Knock[1] knock! Come in.
Open the book, open the door!
Hello, welcome[2] to my new house.
My name's Piggie, the pig.
Moving out, moving in.
Here's my new house,
Isn't it lovely[3]?

(1) knock：敲门。
(2) welcome：欢迎。
(3) lovely：可爱。

房子

● 小猪皮吉自我介绍说："My name's
  Piggie."（我的名字叫皮吉。）模仿皮吉，
  用英语说出自己的名字，"My name's
  ……"。

○ 在英国或美国，向人打招呼时一般会说
  "Hello!"（哈罗！）或"Hi!"（喂！）。
  如果想请别人到你家里去，就会说"Welcome
  to my house!"（欢迎你到我家！）

the chimney
烟囱

the roof
屋顶

the house
房子

the parents'
bedroom
父母的睡房

the bathroom
浴室

the children's
bedroom
孩子的睡房

upstairs
楼上

the bed
床

the living room
客厅

the dining room
饭厅

the kitchen
厨房

the ground floor
地下

the cupboards
橱柜

the table
桌子

wnstairs
楼下

the carpet
地毯

the floor
地板

the chair
椅子

5

What's the weather like?
天气怎样？

the cloud
云

an umbrella
雨伞

It's grey.
天色灰暗。

the wind
风

It's windy.
有风。

the fog
雾

Where are you?
你在哪儿？

It's foggy.
有雾。

It's very windy.
刮大风。

天气怎样？

- 如果想知道今天的天气怎样，可以问 "What's the weather like?"（天气怎样？）对方就会回答："It's foggy, It's rainy, ..."（今天有雾，今天有雨，……）你一边看图，一边用英语说出图中是什么天气。

- 彩虹有几种颜色呢？请用英语说出每种颜色。＊

＊答案：*seven; red, orange, yellow, green, indigo, blue, purple*

It's snowing.
下着雪。

the snow
雪

the winter
冬天

What's the weather like? Is it dry(1)? Is it wet(2)?
What's the weather like? Is it cold? Is it hot?
Let's go and find out!

(1) dry：干燥。
(2) wet：潮湿。

Brrr, it's cold!
呵，真冷！

the rain
雨

It's rainy.
下雨了。

Bye-bye umbrella!
再见雨伞！

the storm
风暴

It's stormy.
有暴风雨。

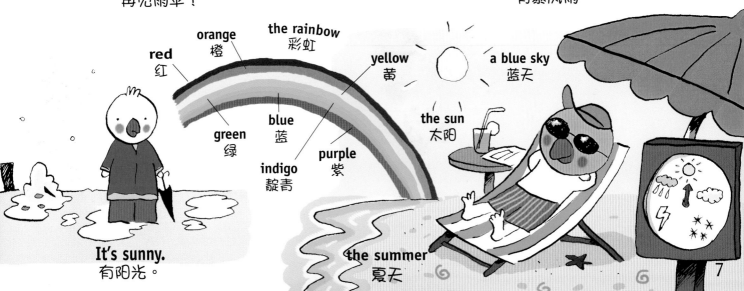

red
红

orange
橙

the rainbow
彩虹

yellow
黄

a blue sky
蓝天

green
绿

blue
蓝

the sun
太阳

indigo
靛青

purple
紫

It's sunny.
有阳光。

the summer
夏天

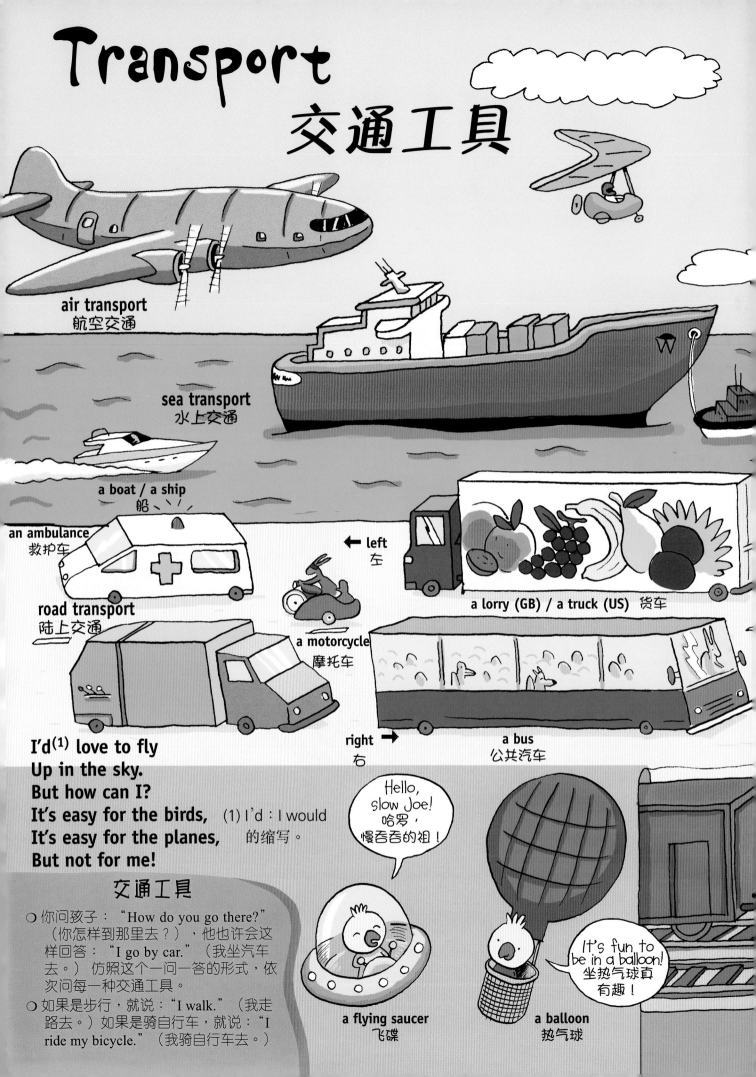

Transport
交通工具

air transport
航空交通

sea transport
水上交通

a boat / a ship
船

an ambulance
救护车

road transport
陆上交通

a motorcycle
摩托车

← left
左

a lorry (GB) / a truck (US) 货车

right →
右

a bus
公共汽车

I'd⁽¹⁾ love to fly
Up in the sky.
But how can I?
It's easy for the birds,   (1) I'd：I would
It's easy for the planes,   的缩写。
But not for me!

Hello,
slow Joe!
哈罗，
慢吞吞的祖！

It's fun to
be in a balloon!
坐热气球真
有趣！

交通工具

○ 你问孩子："How do you go there?"
（你怎样到那里去？），他也许会这
样回答："I go by car."（我坐汽车
去。）仿照这个一问一答的形式，依
次问每一种交通工具。

○ 如果是步行，就说："I walk."（我走
路去。）如果是骑自行车，就说："I
ride my bicycle."（我骑自行车去。）

a flying saucer
飞碟

a balloon
热气球

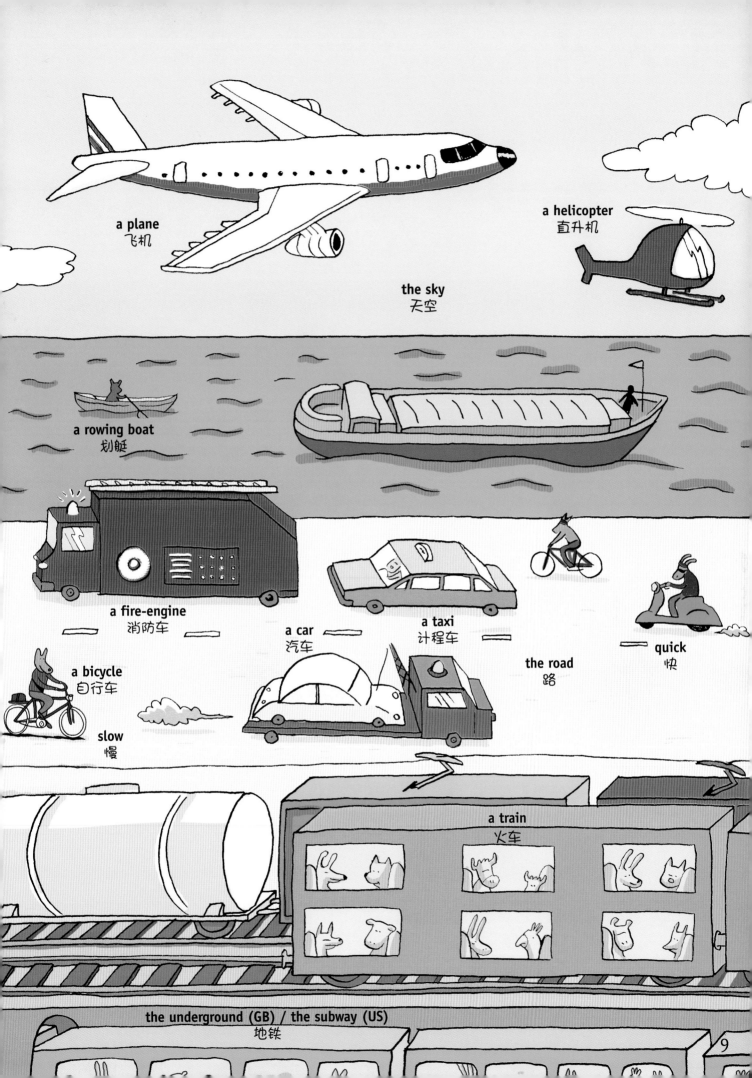

a plane
飞机

a helicopter
直升机

the sky
天空

a rowing boat
划艇

a fire-engine
消防车

a car
汽车

a taxi
计程车

a bicycle
自行车

slow
慢

the road
路

quick
快

a train
火车

the underground (GB) / the subway (US)
地铁

9

Washing 清洗

This little pig is very dirty!
This little pig is going to wash.
Brush and scrub[1], splash[2], splash!
I feel clean as a new pin[3]!

(1) scrub：擦净。
(2) splash：水花飞溅。
(3) clean as a new pin：
　　（惯用语）非常干净。

dirty
肮脏

**wash
清洗**

water
水

hot
热

cold
冷

Wash your hands!
洗手！

the
toothbru
牙刷

**Brush your teeth!
刷牙！**

I'm going to do the washing.
我准备去洗衣服。

So am I!
我也是！

dirty linen
脏衣物

a box
盒子

a bottle
瓶子

**do the washi
洗衣服**

the washing
machine
洗衣机

清洗

● 指着自己身体的某部分（如头部）提问："What is it?"（这是什么？），然后回答说："It is my head."（这是我的头。）仿照这个例子继续提问。

○ 当你想做什么事情时，你就说"I'm going to..."（我要……），例如小狐狸回答说："I'm going to wash my hands."（我要去洗手。）

shampoo
洗发液

wet
湿

the shower
淋浴

head
头

ear
耳

eye
眼

nose
鼻

face
脸

mouth
口

arm
手臂

back
背

elbow
手肘

belly
腹

hand
手

bottom
臀

finger
手指

knee
膝盖

the body
身体

leg
腿

foot / feet
脚

the drier
干衣机

clean
干净

the iron
熨斗

dry
干

11

Counting 数数

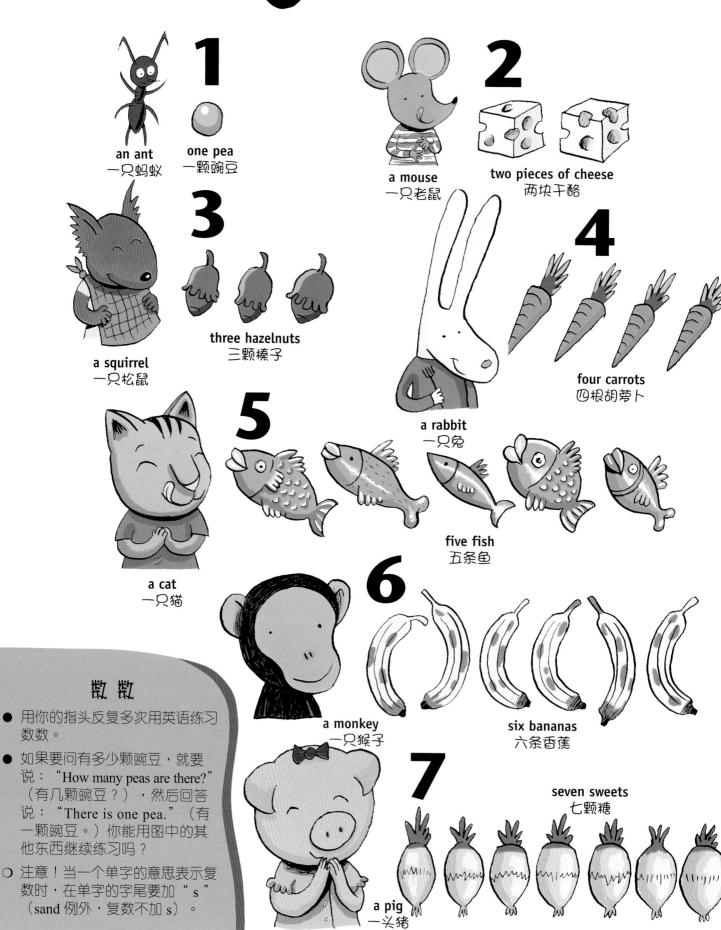

1
an ant
一只蚂蚁

one pea
一颗豌豆

2
a mouse
一只老鼠

two pieces of cheese
两块干酪

3
a squirrel
一只松鼠

three hazelnuts
三颗榛子

4
a rabbit
一只兔

four carrots
四根胡萝卜

5
a cat
一只猫

five fish
五条鱼

6
a monkey
一只猴子

six bananas
六条香蕉

7
seven sweets
七颗糖

a pig
一头猪

数数

- 用你的指头反复多次用英语练习数数。
- 如果要问有多少颗豌豆，就要说："How many peas are there?"（有几颗豌豆？），然后回答说："There is one pea."（有一颗豌豆。）你能用图中的其他东西继续练习吗？
- 注意！当一个单字的意思表示复数时，在单字的字尾要加"s"（sand 例外，复数不加 s）。

8

a cow
一头母牛

eight flowers
八朵花

9

a bear
一只熊

nine honey jars
九瓶蜂蜜

One, two, three,
Suzie mousie,
Is in a hurry[1].
Four, five, six,
Quick, quick,

It's late!
Seven, eight, nine,
Nine o'clock,
Time to dine[2].

(1) in a hurry：
匆忙。
(2) dine：吃晚
饭。

10

an elephant
一头大象

ten sandwiches
十份三文治

11	12	13	14	15	16	17	18	19	20
eleven	twelve	thirteen	fourteen	fifteen	sixteen	seventeen	eighteen	nineteen	twenty

The Forest
森林

a squirrel
松鼠

trees
树

a nest
鸟巢

a bird
鸟

a fox
狐狸

a boar
野猪

animals
动物

grass
草

森林

a mushroom
蘑菇

the bottom
树桩

flowers and plants
花朵和植物

- 在树林里你看见了几种动物？请用英语说出它们的名称。＊
- 指着林中的每一种动物问："What is it?"（这是什么动物？），然后回答说："It's the..."例如："It's the squirrel."（这是松鼠。）

＊答案：*nine; squirrel, bird, fox, boar, owl, snake, deer, rabbit, hedgehog*

the top
树顶

Look! Who's[1] flying?
It's the butterfly.
Listen! Who's
singing?
It's the bird.
Touch! What is it?
It's a rabbit.

(1) who's：who 一般
用来询问人的身份，
但此处是拟人用法。

a branch
树枝

an oak tree
橡树

an owl
猫头鹰

the trunk
树干

a deer
鹿

an ant
蚂蚁

a butterfly
蝴蝶

a hole
洞

wood
木

a rabbit
兔子

a snake
蛇

a leaf
树叶

hedgehog
刺猬

15

Clothes 衣服

the underwear
内衣

bermuda sh
百慕达短裤

a **tracksuit**
运动套装

a **skirt**
裙子

a **jumper (GB) / a sweater (US)**
套头毛衣

a **pock**
口袋

a **cap**
鸭舌帽

a **shirt**
衬衫

panties
内裤

a **scarf**
围巾

a **tee-shirt**
短袖衫

a **hood**
兜帽

trousers (GB) / pants (US)
长裤

summer
夏天

a **hat**
帽子

衣服

- 每个季节中，人们所穿的衣服
  都不同。选一个季节，指着你
  在这个季节里穿的衣服，用英
  语说出它们的名称，例如 "In
  spring, I wear a jacket..."（春
  天我穿夹克……）。

○ 穿衣服的 "穿" 字，用
  "wear"。不要将它和携带某种
  物品的动词 "carry" 混淆了。

spring
春天

a **jacket**
外套

trainers
运动鞋

sungl
太阳

a **bath**
sui
泳

sandals
凉鞋

In the morning,
I jump out of bed
And get dressed(1).

In the evening,
I get undressed
And I jump in bed.
Time to sleep!

(1) get dressed：穿好衣服。

a dress
连身裙

trousers with suspenders
吊带裤

short boots
短靴

trousers
裤

briefs
内裤

a coat
大衣

a windbreaker
风衣

shorts
短裤

a button
钮扣

a raincoat
雨衣

a blouse
女装衬衫

socks
袜

snow boots
雪靴

slippers
拖鞋

autumn / fall
秋天

belt
皮带

an anorak
雪褛

winter
冬天

jeans
牛仔裤

mittens
无指手套

gloves
手套

long boots
长靴

17

The Family 家庭

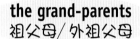 **the grand-parents**
祖父母/外祖父母

the grandmother
外祖母/婆婆

the grandfather
外祖父/公公

Grandma / Granny
祖母/奶奶

Grandpa
祖父/爷爷

the parents
父母

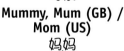

the mother
母亲
**Mummy, Mum (GB) /
Mom (US)**
妈妈

the father
父亲

Daddy / Dad
爸爸

> I like to play cards.
> 我喜欢玩纸牌。

> I do too, but I prefer to win !
> 我也是，不过更喜欢赢啊！

家庭

- 仔细看这两页的图画，辨认这张全家福照片中的人物；指着父亲的样子说："This is the father."（这是父亲。）接着继续说出家中其他人的英语名称。

○ 注意："daughter"的意思是（父母的）"女儿"；而"girl"的意思是"女孩子"，"girl"（女孩子）和"boy"（男孩子）是对应的。

**the children (GB)
the kids (US)**
孩子

the daughter
女儿

the sons
儿子

the sister → **Sam** ← **the brother**
姊妹　　　　萨姆　　　　兄弟

the family picture
全家合照

a baby
婴儿。

Grandma has white hair,
Grandpa has no hair.
Mummy has glasses[1],
And Daddy a long nose.
How about your family?

(1) glasses：眼镜。

the aunt
姑母／姨母

the uncle
姑丈／姨丈

old
年老

young
年轻

the great-grandmother
曾祖母／外曾祖母

the cousin
表兄弟姊妹／堂兄弟姊妹

Sports 运动

a fight
格斗

the belt
腰带

a judoka
柔道选手

judo
柔道

a dancer
舞蹈演员

the floor
舞池

the game
球赛

the ball
球

the racket
球拍

a tournament
锦标赛

> What's your favourite sport?
> 你最爱哪种运动？

> I love running.
> 我爱跑步。

the court
网球场

tennis
网球

training
训练

the helmet
头盔

运动

- 你喜欢哪几种运动？仿照这个例子回答："I like judo, I like dancing…"（我喜欢柔道，我喜欢跳舞……）

- 注意："practice a sport" 的意思是"玩某种运动"，而 "play a game" 的意思是"比赛"，是某种运动的"比赛"。

- 注意：在美国 "soccer" 的意思是 "football"（足球）而 "football" 的意思是（橄榄球），是两种不同的运动。

the bicycle
自行车

bicycle riding
骑自行车

the rider
骑师

the horse
马

jumping
跳跃

horse riding
骑马

Ready? Go!
Ride and swim,
We love it so[1]!
Jump and run,
That's real fun!

(1) so：用以避免
重复上句意思。

dancing
跳舞

the goal
球门

a match / a game
比赛

the net
篮球网

the player
球员

10 | 6

win
胜

lose
负

soccer
足球

basket ball
篮球

swimming
游泳

a swimmer
泳手

goggles
泳镜

3

21

a slide
滑梯

the classroom
课室

painting
涂色

paper
纸

paint
颜料

a student
学生

scissors
剪刀

the caretaker
保姆

the playground
游乐场

the dining hall
食堂

Going to School
上学去

a fork
叉

a napkin
餐巾

a glass
玻璃杯

a knife
刀

上学去

- 现在参观这间幼稚园，并用英语说出你看见的事物的名称，例如看见课室，你就说："This is the classroom."（这是课室。）仿照这个例子继续练习。

- 你知道吗？在英国和美国，放学的时间比较早，下午的时间往往用来进行体育活动。

a picture book 图画书

reading 阅读

the teacher 老师

a letter 字母

playing 玩耍

a pencil 铅笔

the dormitory 宿舍

a bed 床

a blanket 毛毯

School is cool(1)**!**
I paint colours(2)**,**
I learn letters(3)
And numbers.
And you know what?
My teacher
Is a cat!

(1) cool：很棒，很有趣。
(2) paint colours：填颜色。
(3) learn letters：学英文字母。

a plate 碟

a supervisor 舍监

the toilets / rest rooms 洗手间

soap 肥皂

the flush 冲水马桶

the headmistress's office 女校长室

23

Small or Big?
大或小？

I'm so tiny[1],
No one can see me.
Who can I be?
Scratch[2], scratch,
I'm a flea[3],
You see?

(1) tiny：非常小。
(2) scratch：搔痒。
(3) flea：跳蚤。

animals
动物

a tiny louse
非常小的虱子

a small chick
体型细小的
小鸡

a medium size dog
中等大小的狗

a big lion
体型庞大的狮子

plants and trees
植物和树

a tiny seed
一粒小种子

a small tree
一棵矮小的树

a big tree
一棵枝叶茂盛的大树

a tall tree
一棵高高的树

I may be very small, but I can scare an elephant!
或许我个子很小，但我可吓倒大象呢！

fruit
水果

a tiny berry
小浆果

a small banana
小香蕉

a big melon
大甜瓜

a huge coconut
巨型椰子

大或小？

● 看着每一幅图提问："Is the ... big or is it small?"（这……是大还是小？）例如："Is the lion big or is it small?"（这头狮子体型是大还是小？），然后回答："The lion is big."（这头狮子体型庞大。）

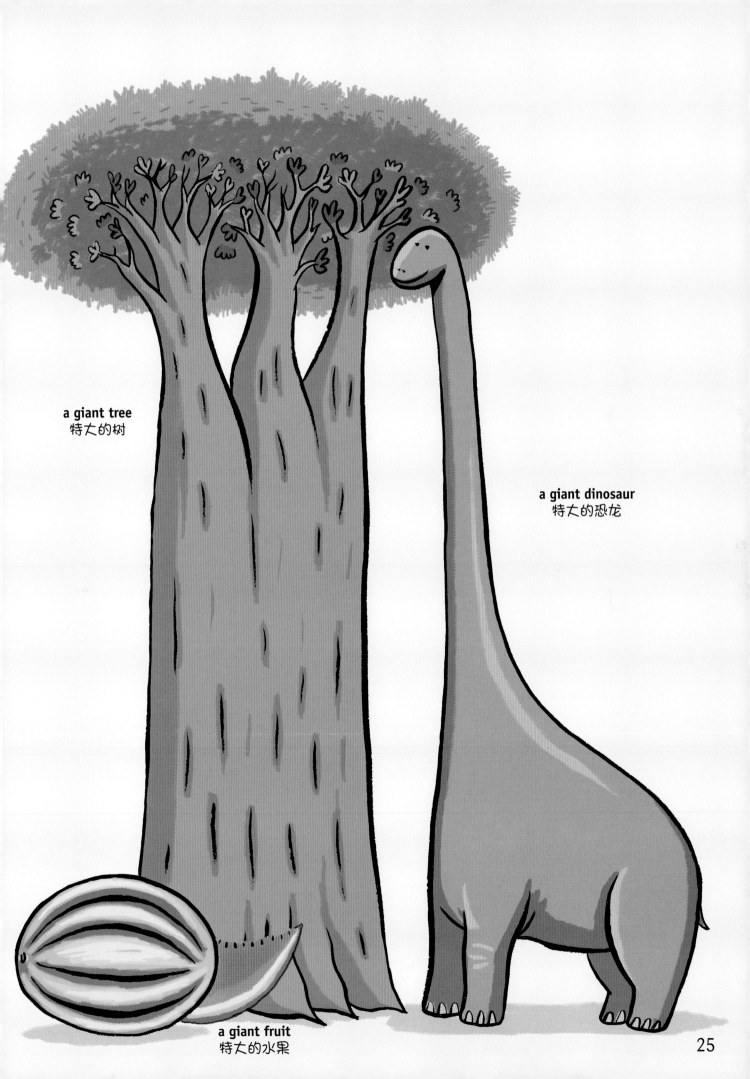

a giant tree
特大的树

a giant dinosaur
特大的恐龙

a giant fruit
特大的水果

Faces and Feelings
面部表情 和感觉

This little bear is happy.
这是快乐的小熊。

This one is sad.
这是伤心的小熊。

This one looks kind.
这是友善的小熊。

Oh, but this one...
哎呀，这只……

... is in a bad mood!
心情不好！

Hello! How are you today?
哈罗！你今天好吗？

Fine, thank you.
好，谢谢你。

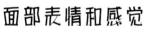

a spotlight
聚光灯

take a picture
拍照

the photographer
摄影师

the camera
照相机

面部表情和感觉

○ 让孩子做出小熊的面部表情，并仿照下列方式提问："Are you tired?"（你累了吗？）"Are you happy?"（你高兴吗？）

○ 孩子回答："Yes, I'm tired."（是，我累了。）或者："No, I'm not tired."（不，我不累。）

This little bear is scared.
这是惊慌的小熊。

And this one is mad.
这是愤怒的小熊。

This other one is surprised.
另外这只小熊表情惊奇。

**What about this one?
He is tired.**
这只怎样？他感到疲倦。

This one is shy.
这是害羞的小熊。

**And the last one is
day-dreaming...**
而最后一只在发白日梦……

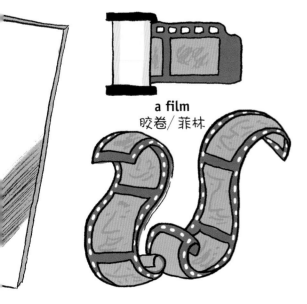

a film
胶卷／菲林

fuzzy
模糊

sharp
清晰

Going to the Mountains 登山

summer
夏天

In the summer,
The mountain
Is a pretty green[1].
But, you know what?
In the winter,
It gets colder and colder,
And it turns all white.

(1) a pretty green : 漂亮的草地。

a glacier
冰川

a river
河

a lake
湖

rock climbing
攀石

a rock
岩石

cows
母牛

hikers
远足者

a bell
铃

meadows
草地

hike
远足

a back-pack
背包

a mountain village
山村

登山

● 在这幅图里有五种不同的下山方法，例如 "I can drive a snow mobile down." （我可以坐摩托雪车下山。）寻找还有哪些方法！*

*答案：*I can ski down./I can snowboard down./I can ride a sledge down./I can drive a snow sweeper down.*

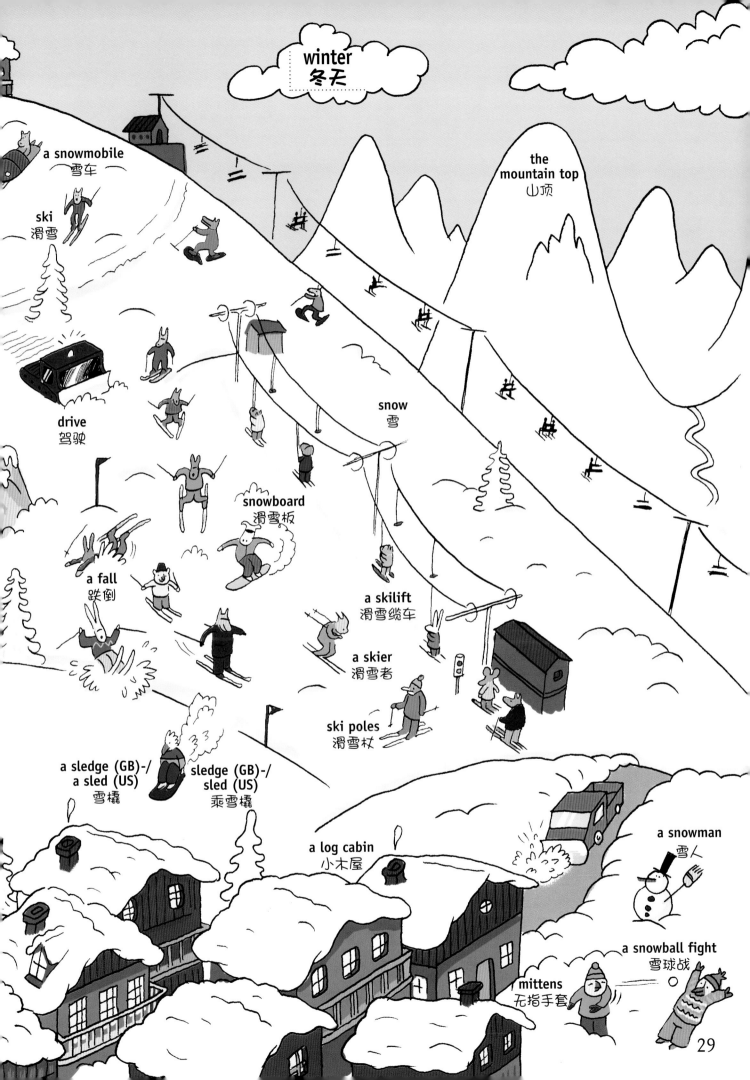

winter
冬天

a snowmobile
雪车

ski
滑雪

the
mountain top
山顶

drive
驾驶

snow
雪

snowboard
滑雪板

a fall
跌倒

a skilift
滑雪缆车

a skier
滑雪者

ski poles
滑雪杖

a sledge (GB)-/
a sled (US)
雪橇

sledge (GB)-/
sled (US)
乘雪橇

a log cabin
小木屋

a snowman
雪人

a snowball fight
雪球战

mittens
无指手套

29

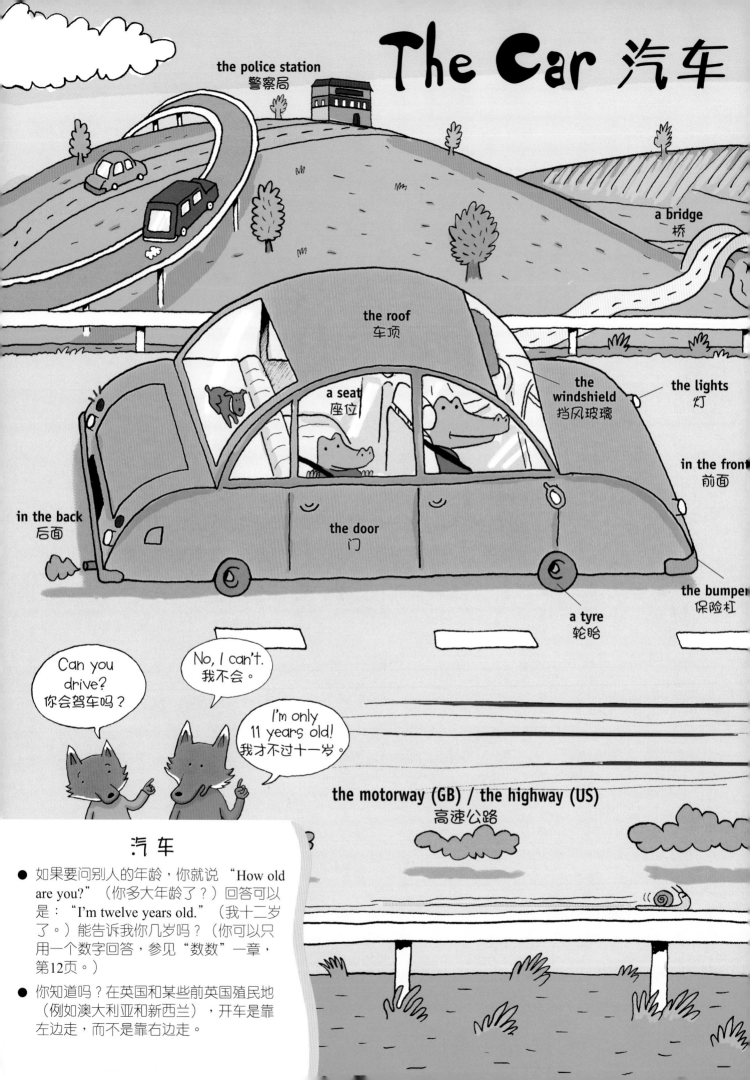

The Car 汽车

the police station 警察局

a bridge 桥

the roof 车顶

a seat 座位

the windshield 挡风玻璃

the lights 灯

in the front 前面

in the back 后面

the door 门

the bumper 保险杠

a tyre 轮胎

Can you drive?
你会驾车吗？

No, I can't.
我不会。

I'm only 11 years old!
我才不过十一岁。

the motorway (GB) / the highway (US)
高速公路

汽车

- 如果要问别人的年龄，你就说 "How old are you?"（你多大年龄了？）回答可以是："I'm twelve years old."（我十二岁了。）能告诉我你几岁吗？（你可以只用一个数字回答，参见"数数"一章，第12页。）

- 你知道吗？在英国和某些前英国殖民地（例如澳大利亚和新西兰），开车是靠左边走，而不是靠右边走。

the toll
收费处

a parking area
停车处

a petrol station (GB)-/
a gas station (US)
油站

Big or small,
Fast or slow,
Red or purple⁽¹⁾,
Green or yellow?
I see them all
Through the window.

(1) purple：紫色。

a road
公路

a passenger
乘客

the driver
司机

drive
驾驶

a convertible
开篷汽车

the steering wheel
方向盘

the gear
变速杆

a baby seat
婴儿座位

a safety belt
安全带

the bonnet (GB)-
the hood (US)
发动机罩盖

the brake
刹车器

the motor
发动机

inside the car
车内

an automatic car
自动变速汽车

31

Pets: Cats and Dogs

the cat
猫

the kitten
小猫咪

the puppy
小狗

the dog
狗

宠物：猫和狗

What do you do?
I jump and mew[1].
Who are you?
I'm a cat.
What do you do?
I eat bones and bark[2].
Who are you?
I'm a dog.

(1) mew：咪咪叫。
(2) bark：吠。

a basket
篮子

sleep
睡觉

a kennel
狗屋

scratch
搔痒

宠物：猫和狗

- 如果要问别人"你在做什么？"，就要说"What are you doing?"例如图中的狗可以回答说"I am catching the ball."（我在抓球。）请看着图回答"What are you doing?"，先代替猫回答，然后代替狗回答。

- "pet"（宠物）可以用来指家养的动物。

purr
呼噜

wag his / her tail
摇尾巴

catch the ball
接球

lap up milk
舔着喝奶

stretch
伸展

play
玩耍

soft
软

sit up
坐直

bark
吠

hard
硬

eat a bone
啃骨头

mew
咪咪叫

rub
擦

bare his /
her teeth
露齿

jump
跳

sniff
嗅

dig a hole
挖洞

round the back
弯着背

bite
咬

a cat-lick
猫儿舔睑

The Playground
游乐场

hide and seek
捉迷藏

run
跑

play tig
捉人

sit in a circle
围圈坐

cops and robbers
兵捉贼

leapfrog
跳背

blind man's buff
蒙着眼捉迷藏

jump
跳

throw
抛

Up and down,
Throw the ball,
Up and down!
Quick, catch(1) it!
Round and round,
Turn until you fall,
Round and round!

(1) catch：接住。

a skipping rope
跳绳用的
绳子

play bowls
玩草地滚球

游乐场

● 如果要问别人"你喜欢什么？"，就要说"What do you like?"。例如图中的鸭子可以回答说"I like to play cops and robbers."（我喜欢玩兵捉贼。）

● 仿照 I like to ... 这个句式，用英语说出你喜欢玩的游戏。

a roundabout
旋转台

hopscotch
跳飞机

a bridge
桥

the see-saw
跷跷板

a slide
滑梯

a swing
秋千

rollerskates
滚轴溜冰鞋

a skateboard
滑板

the sandbox
沙池

a kite
风筝

play ball
玩球

ride a bicycle
骑自行车

a scooter
滑板车

play marbles
玩弹球

35

Cleaning Up 清洁

Little fox,
Yuk(1), yuk!
What did you do?
Silly(2) Billy,
It's all dirty,
Mummy will be very angry(3)!

(1) yuk：表示厌恶的叹词。
(2) silly：傻。
(3) angry：生气。

a broom
扫帚

sweep
扫

pick up
堆起

the dust
尘埃

throw
扔掉

the dustbin (GB) /
the garbage can (US)
垃圾桶

wipe
抹

a dish towel
抹碗布

家务

- 在英语的"vacuum cleaner"（真空吸尘机）里，我们学到了"cleaner"（吸尘机）这个字。现在，你在这两页的图画中找一找，还有哪个字属于"cleaner"这一类。＊

○ 为了帮助孩子记住表示这些动作的名词，你可以把它们编成一首小歌谣，让他跟着你唱："Sweep, sweep, wash, wash, brush, brush, throw, throw ..."（唱名：do, do, mi, mi, so, so, mi, mi）等等。

＊答案：broom。

polish
擦亮

brush
刷

dust
灰尘

the carpet
地毯

scrape
擦掉

the floor
地板

clean
干净

a plate
碟

a bucket
提桶

scrape
擦洗

clean
干净

wash the dishes
洗碗碟

a glass
玻璃杯

put away
收起

the vacuum cleaner
真空吸尘机

polish the floor
擦亮地板

the window
窗

the doormat
门口地垫

dirty
肮脏

37

HOTEL 酒店

BOOKSTORE 书店

a building
建筑物

CAFÉ

a lamp post
灯柱

a crossroads
十字路口
cross
横过

the shop window
商店橱窗

the sidewalk
行人道

FLORIST
花店

On the Street 在街上

forward
向前

← left
左

a pedestrian
行人

the traffic lights
交通灯

a car
汽车

a pram
婴儿车

a motorcyclist
摩托车司机

a bus
公共汽车

Public Garden 公园

在街上

● 指着穿条纹羊毛衫的小狐狸，问 "Where is it?"（它在哪里？），然后回答："It's in..."（它在……里。）＊

● 它要到花店、理发店、肉店、书店和咖啡馆去。我到花店去，英语是 "I'm going to the florist."，仿照 "I'm going to ..." 的句式，说出你要到的地方。

○ 在英语口语里，可以缩短词的形式，如 "he is, she is, it is" 缩短为 "he's, she's, it's"。

＊答案：It's in the public garden. 它在公园里。

SHOE STORE
鞋店

a one way sign
单程路指示牌

roadsigns
交通标志

HAIR DRESSER
理发师

a shop
商店

a lorry (GB) / a truck (US)
货车

butcher
肉贩

BU

a zebra crossing
斑马线

TOWN CENTRE
市中心

a bench
长凳

Whizz[1], whizz:
a car to the left,
a car to the right,
Honk[2], honk: a bus to the
left, a bus to the right,
Vroom, vroom[3]: a
motorcycle
In front, a lorry behind.
Here and there, watch out[4]!
The street's very busy.

a square
广场

(1) whizz：急速的声音。
(2) honk：汽车喇叭声。
(3) vroom：轰隆声。
(4) watch out：小心。

What I love...
我爱……

I love sweets and chocolate[1],
I love running and laughing,
I love playing and jumping.
But guess[2] what I love most...
I can't tell you, it's a secret[3]!

(1) chocolate：
巧克力。
(2) guess：猜。
(3) secret：秘密。

I love...
我爱……

...rolling in the grass and having a good laugh.
……在草地上翻滚并开怀大笑。

...sticking my finger in the chocolate cream.
……用我的手指沾上巧克力奶油。

...staying in bed when it's
time to go to school.
……在该上学时仍留在
床上睡觉。

...making faces in
front of the mirror.
……在镜子前面
扮鬼脸。

...making soap bubbles.
……吹肥皂泡泡。

...blowing thistle flowers.
……吹蒲公英。

...messing up
with mud.
……在泥泞中玩
到满身脏。

...jumping right
into a puddle.
……跳入水洼中。

我爱……

○ 在动词"like"和"love"后面，
接另一个动词的"-ing"形式造
句，例如："I like drawing, I like
eating, I like playing."（我喜欢
画画，我喜欢吃，我喜欢玩。）
仿照"I like -ing 动词"的句式，
用英语说你喜欢做的事情。

...smelling pancakes.
……嗅薄饼的香味。

...imagining animals when I look at clouds.
……当看见云，我把它想像为动物。

...swearing and running away.
……骂人后逃走。

...giving a nice big hug.
……来个令人愉快的深深的拥抱。

...letting icecubes melt in my mouth.
……让冰块在我口中溶化。

...hiding under the eiderdown to read a good book.
……躲在羽绒被下面看一本好书。

...drawing on a misty window.
……在有雾气的窗上画画。

...having a feast on bread and jam.
……尽情地吃面包配果酱。

...trampling dead leaves to make a lot of noise.
……践踏枯叶弄出许多噪音。

...grabbing my presents and tearing off the wrapping paper.
……收到礼物后撕开包装纸。

41

On the Beach
在海滩上

Take your bucket and
take your spade,
Let's build castles on the sand.
Here come the waves, quick, quick!
Too late! My beautiful castle
tumbles down[1].

(1) tumbles down：倒塌。

windsurfing
滑浪风帆

a float
浮床

sunglass
太阳眼镜

a seagull
海鸥

scuba diving
徒手潜水

the sea
海

You're red as a lobster!
你红得像只龙虾！

I'm getting a sunburn.
我给晒伤了。

a bucket
提桶

a sandcastle
沙堆城堡

the sand
沙

a spa[de]
铲子

seaweeds
海草

a cap
鸭舌帽

a parasol
太阳伞

sunlotion
防晒液

在海滩上

● 看着图，用英语说"干的"(dry)
和"湿的"(wet)。就一件物品或
一只动物提问："What is dry?"
（什么是干的？）回答："This
towel is dry."（这条毛巾是干
的。）你接着又问："What is
wet?"（什么是湿的？）回答：
"This pig is wet."（这头猪浑身
是湿的。）

○ 注意：如果就一个人提问，就要
说"Who's dry/wet?"（谁浑身是
干的/湿的？）

a sailboat
帆船

a kite
风筝

waves
浪

a life-saver
救生员

swimmers
泳客

a rubber ring
救生圈

a beach towel
沙滩巾

the
ice-cream
seller
冰淇淋
小贩

seashells
贝壳

a sandal
凉鞋

the beach
沙滩

a crab
蟹

rocks
石头

wet
湿

dry
干

Celebrations 节日庆祝

"Trick(1) or treat(2)?"
Can you repeat it?
"Trick or treat?"
"Give me some
sweets, And
I won't play
any tricks."

(1) trick：捣蛋。
(2) treat：请客。

a birthday party
生日会

the guests
宾客

balloons
气球

candles
蜡烛

a straw
吸管

sweets (GB) /
candies (US)
糖果

fruit juice
果汁

a piece of cake
一块蛋糕

a birthday cake
生日蛋糕

a paper cup
纸杯

a paper
plate
纸碟

At Christmas,
we get presents, but for
Halloween we get sweets.
圣诞节我们收到礼物，但万
圣节前夕我们
收到糖果。

Halloween
万圣节前夕

costumes
服装

a pumpkin
南瓜

a ghost
鬼

masks
面具

a witch
女巫

an E.T.
外星人

节日庆祝

● 在庆祝万圣节时，孩子们挨家去敲门，一边叫着"Trick or treat?"，一边伸手要糖果。在圣诞节和新年，见到人就说："Merry Christmas and Happy New Year!"（圣诞快乐！新年快乐！）

● 如果表示"想要什么东西"，你就说"I'd like..."。例如"I'd like fruit juice, please."（请给我果汁。）

Christmas Eve
平安夜

lights
灯饰

decorations
装饰物

Santa Claus
圣诞老人

a sled
雪橇

a star
星

garlands
花环状
饰物

the snow
雪

presents / gifts
礼物

a Christmas tree
圣诞树

the Carnival's parade
嘉年华巡游

fireworks
烟花

firecrackers
爆竹

a Chinese
lantern
中式灯笼

A wild animal at home,
That's my dream!
Take my bath with a hippo ,
Play with a monkey,
And run with a lion,
That would be[2] so much fun!

(1) hippo：河马。
(2) would be：表示假想中现在发生的事。

an elephant
大象

the Tse Tse fly
采采蝇

a herd
一群

a monkey
猴子

a black panther
黑豹

a rhino
犀牛

a giraffe
长颈鹿

a scorpio
蝎子

a gorilla
大猩猩

a lynx
山猫

a zebra
斑马

a cheetah
猎豹

a leopard
豹

a common goral
斑羚

47

Shopping at the Supermarket

在超级市场购物

ICE-CREAM 冰淇淋

PIZZA 薄饼

canned food 罐头食品

PASTA 意大利面　RICE 米

advertising 广告

FROZEN FOOD 冷藏食品

My purse[1]'s full of money,
But my basket's empty.
Shop[2], shop, shop!
Look, now, my
basket's full...
But my purse's empty!

(1) purse：钱包。
(2) shop：购物。

CLEANING PRODUCTS 清洁用品

a cashier 收银员

money 钱

4

3 -10

queue up 排队

plastic bags 胶袋

cash register 收银机

在超级市场购物

- 要买胡萝卜时，就说："I need carrots."（我要买胡萝卜。）按左边的购物清单，指着要买的东西，继续用 "I need ..." 说出来。

  i. rice（米）
  ii. frozen food（冷藏食品）
  iii. meat（肉类）
  iv. pasta（意大利面）
  v. fruit（水果）
  vi. bread（面包）

- 把单字排成一对一对地学，便更容易学会。例如 "full"（满）和 "empty"（空）。帮助孩子找出可以成对学习的英语单字。✱

✱建议答案：意义相反的如 the entrance, the exit；与金钱有关的如 money, the price 等等。

the price
价钱

DAIRY PRODUCTS 奶类制品　DRINKS 饮品

MEAT 肉　　FISH 鱼

a tag
标签

FRUIT 水果　　VEGETABLES 蔬菜

the customers
顾客

full
满

a trolley (GB) /
a caddie (US)
手推车

a counter
柜台

empty
空

the exit
出口

the baskets
购物篮

the entrance
入口

49

Fruit and Vegetables
水果和蔬菜

a pear
梨

a mango
芒果

a peach
桃

a nectarine
油桃

a banana
香蕉

But where's my apple?
我的苹果在哪里？

olives
橄榄

a melon
甜瓜

a grapefruit
西柚

a Clementine
小柑橘

a fig
无花果

an orange
橙

Lovely(1) and juicy(2),
That's the cherry!
Red and tasty(3),
What could it be?
I bet(4) it's the strawberry.

(1) lovely：可爱。
(2) juicy：多汁。
(3) tasty：好味道。
(4) I bet：我敢肯定。

a cauliflower
花椰菜

string beans
四季豆

peas
豌豆

an eggplant
矮瓜

a leek
韭葱

hot pepper
辣椒

peppers
甜椒

水果和蔬菜

● 以下是一日三餐的表达法：

i. "I eat my breakfast in the morning."（我早上吃早餐。）

ii. "I eat lunch at noon."（我中午吃午餐。）

iii. "I eat a snack in the afternoon."（我下午吃点心。）

iv. "I eat dinner in the evening."（我晚上吃晚餐。）

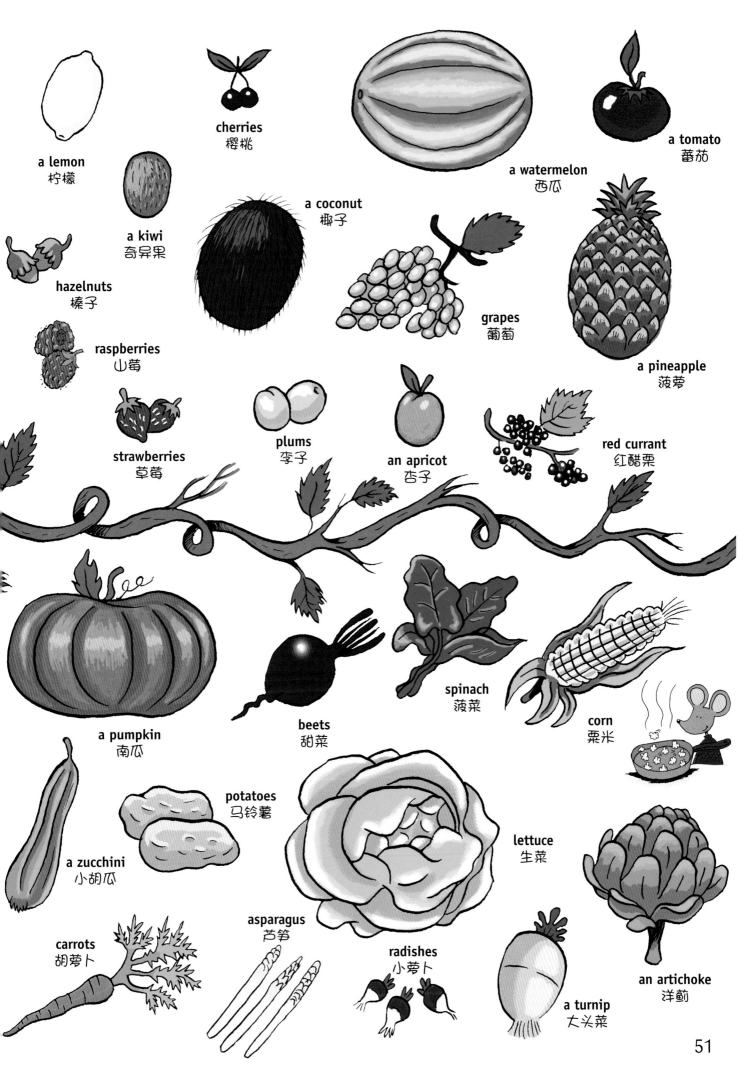

a lemon
柠檬

cherries
樱桃

a watermelon
西瓜

a tomato
蕃茄

a kiwi
奇异果

a coconut
椰子

grapes
葡萄

a pineapple
菠萝

hazelnuts
榛子

raspberries
山莓

strawberries
草莓

plums
李子

an apricot
杏子

red currant
红醋栗

a pumpkin
南瓜

beets
甜菜

spinach
菠菜

corn
粟米

potatoes
马铃薯

lettuce
生菜

a zucchini
小胡瓜

asparagus
芦笋

radishes
小萝卜

a turnip
大头菜

an artichoke
洋蓟

carrots
胡萝卜

51

The Farm
农场

the fence 篱笆

the cows 母牛

the donkey 驴子

the goat 山羊

the sheep 绵羊

hay 干草

the barn 谷仓

a calf 小牛

the turkey 火鸡

the goose 鹅

eggs 蛋

the chicks 小鸡

the farmer 农夫

the duck 鸭

农场

○ 表示"有"或"拥有"用 "I've got"（have got 的缩写 形式）。例如：农场主人说 "I've got cows."（我有许多头 母牛。）在疑问句中，要把主 语和动词的次序颠倒过来说： "Have you got any cows?" （你有母牛吗？）

● 仿照这个例子，问农场主人有 没有某种动物，然后回答。例 如："Have you got any cows? Yes, I've got cows."（你有母 牛吗？有，我有多头母牛。）

a field
田

the stable
马房

the horse
马

the cat
猫

the dog
狗

the mouse
老鼠

the rooster
公鸡

a tractor
拖拉机

the hen
母鸡

the pig
猪

the rabbit
兔

Hello Cow,
Have you got
Any milk for me?
Moo[1], moo!
Yes, I do,
It's nice and
creamy[2],
And it's all for you!

(1) moo：牛叫声。
(2) creamy：嫩滑。

53

Jobs 职业

a builder
泥水匠

a teacher
老师

$$1 + 1 = 2$$

a fireman
消防员

a carpenter
木匠

the saw
锯

the hammer
锤子

the petrol station (GB) / the gas station (US)
油站

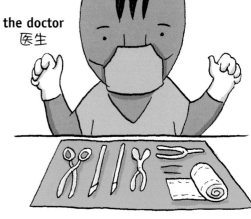

the doctor
医生

a pair of scissors
一把剪刀

a computer programmer
电脑程式设计员

a hairdresser
理发师

职 业

- 你知道吗？在英国和美国，十几岁的孩子可以找到送报纸、替邻居看管动物或修剪草坪等小差事做，借此来赚点钱。

○ 指男人用 "he" （他），指女人用 "she" （她），指动物或物品用 "it" （它）。

a fisherman
渔夫

a singer
歌手

a movie camera
电影摄录机

a cameraman
摄影师

the cash register
收银机

the baker
面包师傅

bread
面包

a policeman
警察

a gun
枪

change
零钱

a shop assistant
店员

the thermometer
温度计

a bee keeper
养蜂人

bees
蜜蜂

a nurse
护士

honey
蜜糖

a greedy
little bear
贪心的小熊

a sculptor
雕刻家

When I'm older,
I wonder(1), wonder
What my job will be.
Will I be a doctor?
Will I be a teacher?
Or will I be a baker
In a bakery(2)?

(1) wonder：自问。
(2) bakery：面包店。

55

Going Out
上街去

Up and over,
Down and under,
Round and round,
Upside down,
Hold on tight[1]!

(1) hold on tight：抓紧。

the screen
银幕

a film
电影

the cinema / the pictures
电影院

the audience
观众

the seats
座位

the usher
引座员

Ice-cream, pop corn.
冰淇淋，爆米花。

a spotlight
聚光灯

the set
布景

the puppet show
木偶戏

the curtain
帷幕

the puppets
木偶

people clapping
观众拍掌

上街去

- "Today I'm going to the pictures." 的意思是"今天我要去看电影。"仿照"Today I'm going to ..."句式，说去看木偶戏，去看马戏，去逛市集！

- 你知道吗？英国和美国的孩子们都看过潘奇 (Punch) 和朱迪 (Judy) 这两个木偶的表演。这两个木偶遇到了各种各样不幸的事情。

the circus
马戏团

the circus tent
马戏团帐篷

a lion
狮子

the circus ring
马戏场

the performing
artists
表演者

the clowns
小丑

acrobats
杂技演员

the tiers
一排排座位

the funfair
露天游乐场

the big wheel
摩天轮

a merry-go-round
旋转木马

a trailer
掩车

a ghost train
鬼车

SWEETS
糖果

dodgems
碰碰车

candy floss
棉花糖

fishing
钓鱼

Opposites

反义词

I say Hello,
She says Goodbye!
If I'm here,
It's daylight[1].
If I'm there,
Your eyes are shut tight.
And it's night.
Who is she? Who am I?*

(1) daylight : 白天。

* 我是太阳，她是月亮。

laugh
笑

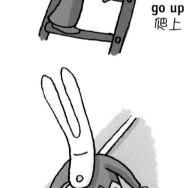

cry
哭

go up
爬上

go down
下来

warm up
取暖

cool off
降温

start
开始

finish
完成

listen
聆听

speak
说话

catch
接

反义词

请注意几对正反标示符号：

on ⏻ - off ⭘
开 - 关

up↑ - down↓
上 - 下

in ▣ - out □▪
在里面 - 在外面

over ▫ - under ▫
在上边 - 在下边

front ▣ - back □▪
在前面 - 在后面

throw
抛

shout
大声叫

whisper
低声说

get wet
弄湿

get dry
弄干

do
扣上钮扣

undo
解开钮扣

go forward
前进

go backward
后退

get messy
弄脏

wash up
清洗

get up
起床

go to bed
上床睡觉

wind up
卷起

unwind
展开

59

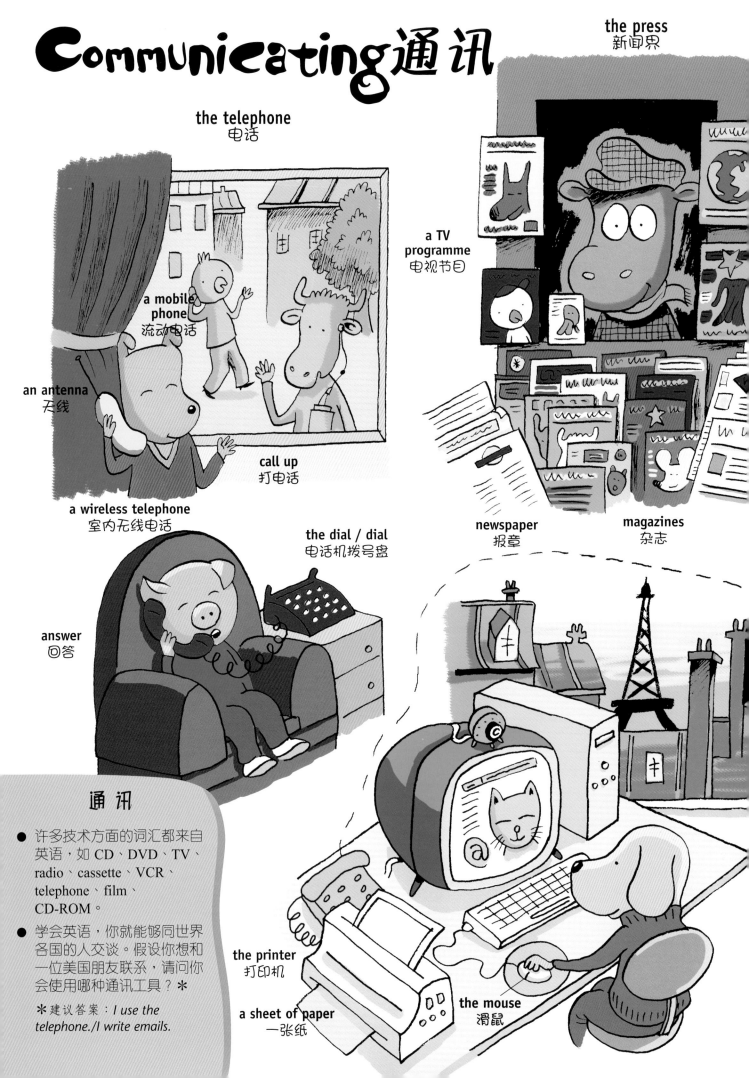

Communicating 通讯

the press
新闻界

the telephone
电话

a mobile phone
流动电话

an antenna
天线

call up
打电话

a TV programme
电视节目

a wireless telephone
室内无线电话

the dial / dial
电话机拨号盘

answer
回答

newspaper
报章

magazines
杂志

通讯

● 许多技术方面的词汇都来自英语，如 CD、DVD、TV、radio、cassette、VCR、telephone、film、CD-ROM。

● 学会英语，你就能够同世界各国的人交谈。假设你想和一位美国朋友联系，请问你会使用哪种通讯工具？✻

✻建议答案：*I use the telephone./I write emails.*

the printer
打印机

a sheet of paper
一张纸

the mouse
滑鼠

a computer
电脑

email
电子邮件

the screen
屏幕

a CD-ROM
唯读光碟

the keyboard
键盘

A, B, C, D,
Listen to the CD
E, F, G, H, I, J,
Can you play?
K, L, M, N, O, P,
Lovely!
Q, R, S, T, U, V,
Let's watch TV
W, X, Y, Z
Let's go to bed
Instead(1)!

(1) instead：代替。

television and hi-fi
电视和音响组合

a compact disc (CD)
光碟

a radio and cassette player
卡式收音机

a CD player
光碟播放机

a video cassette recorder (VCR)
录影机

videocassette
式录影带

a digital video record (DVD)
数码影碟

the remote control
遥控器

an earphone
耳机

61

English-Chinese Topic Index
英汉主题索引

Festival and entertainment
节日及娱乐

Nature: countryside, mountains
大自然：郊外，山岭

Landscape 风景

Weather / season
天气 / 季节

Animal, bird and insect
动物、鸟及昆虫

House, Town
房子，城市

House 房子